舞動心弦

與佛陀談情說愛

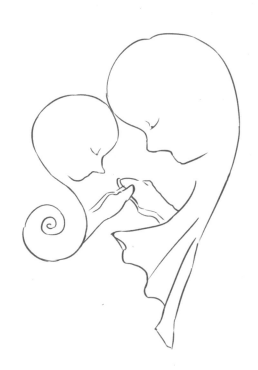

Dancing in My Heart

Romancing the Buddha

Tina Ho 何曼盈

Before

2016 年 6 月我和數位同修應阿南渡登仁波切的邀請，飛往三藩市的海岸區，在著名的大蘇爾（Big Sur）森林區，參加一至兩星期的個人閉關⋯⋯

In June 2016, several other classmates and I accepted Rinpoche's invitation to join a solitary retreat in California's famous Big Sur forest⋯⋯

▲Coast line in Big Sur 大蘇爾區海岸綫

◀

Dana
(Caretaker's office)

看守員辦公室

▼Buddha status near Dana 佛像

► Shila (cabin)

小屋

► Bathhouse and bridge
  near Nirvana Road

澡堂及木橋

▼Ksanti (cabin) and Śūnyatā (yurt)　小屋及蒙古包

Wonderful resting time 美好的休息時間

After Fire

2016 年 7 月下旬，加州森林大火漫延此地，
一切的可能性亦因此次山火而躍動。

In late July 2016, the wildfires that had been
raging in California had found Sweetwater. New
possibilities are born with every death.

▲Dana the caretaker's office is razed by the fire.
看守員辦公室被焚燬

▼Prajñā (cabin) and the surrounding environment have been repairing.
小屋及附近環境進行修復中

▲Quan Yin (Avalokitesvara) prevailed through the fire
and is now surrounded by spring.

觀音被火洗禮，現在被春天簇擁

Spring & Sunflower
Flowers return to earth.

花兒重臨人間

◄

Photo by Bodhi
Sangho Shin

Content 目錄

Preface

Life is full of mystery. We never know who we're going to run into. Tomorrow you might run into someone who is going to be a good friend. This was what happened to me. Three years ago, I didn't know that Tina existed on this planet. She came to my very first meditation retreat in Hong Kong in 2014. Since then, we keep running into each other and have become good friends. I find her a very courageous and compassionate person. She is also a wonderful writer and performer.

Tina knows that I love reading poems. She often writes poems and sends them to me. Her poems come from the heart and they express where she is on her life's journey, along with her insight, love, devotion and other rich human experiences. They have the power to move us and invoke those experiences in us. She wrote them with a deep sincerity that makes each poem precious and personal. Though she's well read in Buddhist philosophy, her poems are not intellectual at all. She doesn't use jargons in these poems that describe her relationship with the Buddhist path. I regard her as a modern Zen poet for some reason, whether or not she finds this a compliment.

This world needs poems as much as it needs flowers and music. It would be much lonelier if these don't exist. The new poetry book by

Tina is a beautiful flower that brings the magic of joy to this world. There is nothing better than to have a poetry book on the night stand. It can be the delicious chocolate you enjoy and share with your friends. If you're looking for something to put on your night stand, you may like this lovely book that will keep you company and make your heart grow wider.

Anam Thubten

序

　　生命如此奧妙，我們無法預知將會與誰相遇。也許明天你可能會遇到一位將成為你的摯友的人。這是我切身的經歷。三年之前，我不知道 Tina 存在於這個星球上。2014 年，她到來參加我首次在香港舉辦的禪修閉關營，從那時候開始，我倆持續交往，成為好友。我覺得她是一位非常勇敢和富有慈悲心的人，她也是一位優秀的作家和表演者。

　　Tina 知道我熱愛詩詞，她時常寫詩，並轉寄給我。她的詩詞發自她的內心及反映她在當下人生階段的心路歷程，分享她的洞見、愛、虔敬心以及透過她豐富的人生體驗而有的切身感悟，它們具有感染力，也引起我們的共鳴。Tina 創作的詩源於她真誠的流露，故此每首詩都顯得份外珍貴和洋溢着她心底裏的真情實感。雖然她飽讀精通佛家哲學，但是她的詩作並不帶學術性，沒有運用很多專門述語來描寫她和成佛之道的關係。無論她是否認為這是讚美，我會把她看成是一位現代的禪意詩人。

　　這個世界需要詩，如同需要花和音樂一樣，如果這些都不存在，我們將會非常寂寞。Tina 這本新詩集是一朵美麗的花兒，為這個世界帶來一種神奇的喜悅。沒有什麼比在床架上置放一本詩集來的更好。它像是你與你的朋友共享的美味巧克力。如果你正在尋找一些東西放在你的床架上，也許你會喜歡這本優美的作品，它將陪伴着你，並讓你的心變得更遼濶。

（翻譯自英文）

阿南渡登

Translator's preface

When at first Tina invited me to translate some of her poems, I hesitated saying yes. Translating poetry from English to Chinese isn't easy; too often, the translation fails to fully capture the mood of the poem, or even what the poet means to say. But after reading her work and finding out that the project is aimed at raising funds for the rebuilding of the fire-ravaged Sweetwater Sanctuary retreat center, I gladly agreed to do my part. And I have tried my best to render in Chinese not just the unique tone of Tina's voice, but also the pure innocence of her feelings.

Most of the poems in this collection related Tina's experiences in Sweetwater. They flow naturally from the depths of her heart, these songs of praise and prayer that reflect her devotion to her guru, the Buddha and dharma. Reading them, we are transported to Sweetwater, before it was ravaged by the fire. Immersed in its wooded serenity and beauty everywhere, our spirits are refreshed. The brutal flames that swept through the woods may have destroyed Sweetwater, but the workings of impermanence have also given the sanctuary new life. As we wait to see the rebirth of Sweetwater, we can remember what it used to be and celebrate the beauty it has left behind through these poems.

All beings that are born will grow old, get sick and die. But our innate compassion and wisdom are indestructible.

Through these poems, we, too, may romance the Buddha. Through them, we feel the unconditional love our guru – the teacher who leads us towards the path of liberation – offers us. Such love awakens the ocean of love in our own hearts, inspiring kindness for all, and acceptance of all that life brings.

(Translated from Chinese)

Brian Tee
Freelance writer & columnist
19-8-2017
Kuala Lumpur, Malaysia

譯者序

　　記得當曼盈邀請我為她著作的詩做翻譯的時候，我心中泛起了遲疑，原因是要把用英文寫的詩翻譯成中文並不是件容易的事，一個不留意，詩的意境和本意就會被削弱而喪失了作者所想要表達的情感。只可是，在看了她的詩過後，也了解她想要出版這本詩集的目的是為了被森林野火摧毀的甜水鄉禪林（Sweetwater Sanctuary）籌募重建資金，我也無法拒絕而欣然接下了翻譯的重任，盡可能將曼盈詩句裏本有的個性和純真的情感以中文去呈獻。

　　曼盈在這本詩集裏大部份記錄了她在甜水鄉閉關時的一些體驗和經歷，也包括了她對上師、佛、以及佛法的虔誠心，用她心底裏自然流露的情感以詩句頌念吟唱。閱讀曼盈的詩仿如置身於甜水鄉，感受徜徉在還沒有被野火摧毀的那一片寧靜的叢林裏，沉浸在那美麗的點點滴滴，洗滌着心靈。也許，無情的火焰已將甜水鄉摧毀，只可是，無常卻也為它賦予了全新的生命，在期待着甜水鄉全新面貌的展現之同時，讓我們共同以曼盈的這本詩集去悼念甜水鄉以往的面貌和留下的美麗。

　　所有的事物必有生、住、壞、滅、而不被摧毀的依然是那份本具的慈愛與智慧。

　　我們也可以借助曼盈在詩集裏的詩去與佛談一場交心的戀愛，去感受導引我們通往解脫之道的上師給予我們的那一份無條件的愛，來喚醒我們內在深處的那一片愛的海洋，去包容萬事萬物，去慈愛所有的一切。

蘇悅
自由撰稿人、專欄作家
寫於　吉隆坡　馬來西亞
2017 年 8 月 19 日

A Chance Encounter

From the beginning of that chance encounter
You unfold your life
Searching for and rebuilding your spirit

Head to head
It shook you up
Unlocked your shackles
Released your fears
How deep and true is this realization,
And so peaceful!

You
Love to listen to the blue birds singing
Love to see the deer glancing back
Love the tranquility of Sweetwater
It is a spiritual paradise
There you can sing loudly
There you can chant quietly
There you can burst into a run
Or aimlessly wander
You can lie on the redwood bench

邂逅

從一次邂逅開始，
妳開展妳那生命的重索、心靈的重修。

頭碰頭的震撼，
解開妳的枷鎖，
釋放妳的恐懼。
那是一種多麼深、多麼真、多麼空靜的感悟！

妳
愛聽那青鳥的鳴聲、
愛看那小鹿的回眸、
更愛甜水鄉的靈靜。
那是一片心靈的樂土，
妳可在那高聲放歌、低聲誦念、
也可在那放足前奔、卻步徘徊。
又或躺在那紅木板凳上賞月數星。

一切是
原始的、
平和的、
仁愛的、

Watching the moon
And counting the stars

A primordial scene where
Everything is at peace
Loving and compassionate

You
Are no longer afraid of goodbyes
At the moment your fingertips meet
You and your heart guru are one
One breath breathing in
One breath breathing out
Step forward and back
Left and right
Up and down
Push and pull
All is in harmony
All is wonderful
Just like your name
You are dancing in the Buddha pure land

(Translated from Chinese)

Chan Ka Ling
 (author's class teacher in secondary school)

慈悲的。

妳
不再害怕離別，
在指尖相連的一刻
妳的心已和上師相融，
呼與吸已和上師同步……
一前一後
一左一右
一上一下
一拖一拉
是如斯的合拍、
如斯的美妙！
如同妳的名字
於佛國淨土中曼舞輕盈……

陳家玲
（作者中學班主任）

Author's preface

While catching up with a former secondary school classmate one afternoon about four years ago, I told her how much I was enjoying the practice of meditation under the guidance of my teacher, Yongey Mingyur Rinpoche. My friend Ivy didn't know much about the Buddha or Buddhism, but she sensed my joy, and teasingly said that I seemed to be romancing the Buddha. Her quip became the subtitle of this poetry collection.

I first met Anam Thubten Rinpoche about three years ago. Rinpoche, who has lived in America for more than 20 years, is not only a Buddha dharma lineage holder, but also a poet. Under his influence, I began to write poems and share them with friends. I attended Rinpoche's teachings and meditation retreats whenever I could. In that time, I got to know him, and his teachings, so full of humility and unconditional love, awakened my heart. "Dancing in my heart" is a phrase Rinpoche often uses; thanks to his guidance, my heart, too, has begun to dance.

In June 2016, several other classmates and I accepted Rinpoche's invitation to join a solitary retreat in California's famous Big Sur forest. For three days there, Rinpoche shared his precious teachings with us. In this sanctuary named Sweetwater, my constant companions were the majestic redwoods, the turkey vultures soaring overhead, the deer in the woods, and the fence lizards sunning themselves on the rocks. During those two weeks of "forest meditation", I grew to appreciate life's simplicity and tasted such deep contentment that I felt as though I were living in the Pure Land. I am grateful for Rinpoche's compassionate blessings, so that I was able to learn this precious lesson.

After I came back to Hong Kong in early July, I began to write many poems about my experience at the retreat. These poems were guided by a pure and selfless love, and inspired by the pulse of life itself. Awareness of the present moment is a gift indeed. Gratitude fills my heart like nectar, and I offer it to the immeasurably kind and compassionate Buddha. In late July, I saw photos on Facebook that showed the skies above our sanctuary awash with orange, and learned that the wildfires that had been raging in California had found Sweetwater. After the fire came the floods. Rinpoche wrote a poem acknowledging life's uncertainty, pointing out the new possibilities that are born with every death, and urging us to "stay with the not knowing".

The publication of this poetry collection stems from a wish to make a contribution, however meagre, to the rebuilding of this precious retreat center. None of this would have been possible without the support of the publisher Mr Lai, who kindly agreed to design and print this little book at cost, and two friends, TC and Brian, who helped, respectively, to edit the poems and translate them from English to Chinese, making the poems more expressive than I could have made them on my own. I owe them all a debt of thanks. My deepest gratitude goes out to my beloved teacher and good friend, Anam Thubten Rinpoche. Thanks to the coming together of many causes and conditions, I have had the opportunity to join many of Rinpoche's teachings and retreats, both in Hong Kong and Malaysia, over the past three years, and received so much of his encouragement and support. Thank you, for making this book of poems possible, and for making my life richer and more colorful than ever before.

My gratitude goes to Professor Andrew Chan, Ms Chan Ka Ling and Brian for their kind words about the poems. In their own way, each of them suggests how an encounter with the Buddha can be a doorway for an inward journey, towards the discovery of an innate love that is completely open and unconditional, and a pure joy that echoes in all our hearts. Lastly, I must thank my family in Hong Kong and the US, as well as my friends from the Dharmata Foundation in America, Malaysia and Hong Kong. Their support and encouragement over the past three years made it possible for me to attend teachings and retreats with great peace of mind. I pray that all of you may one day visit Sweetwater, to see for yourselves its ancient forestlands and find there a doorway into the sacred. (Translated from Chinese)

Tina Ho

27-8-2017

Hong Kong

作者序

　　大約 4 年以前的一個下午，我和一位舊中學同學 Ivy，分享我跟隨上師詠給‧明就仁波切學習禪修的喜悅，她對佛陀和佛教都沒有太多認識，但她感受到我內心的歡欣，更笑言我和佛陀在拍拖，這個風趣的回應，竟成為了這本詩集的副題。

　　最近 3 年認識了定居美國 20 多年的阿南渡登仁波切，他是一位佛法的持有者，也是一位詩人，在他的薰陶下我開始以詩會友。參加他的禪修營和聆聽他的教法，讓我感受到他的謙虛和內心無條件的愛，並喚醒了我的心，舞動心弦（Dancing in My Heart）便是他經常會用來描寫他的心境的文詞，潛移默化的引導下，亦成為了我內心的反照。

　　去年 6 月我和數位同修應阿南渡登仁波切的邀請，飛往三藩市的海岸區，在著名的大蘇爾（Big Sur）森林區，參加一至兩星期的個人閉關，其中三天他更親自給予寶貴的開示。在這個幽靜的甜水鄉（Sweetwater），參天的紅木、翱翔藍天的雄鷹、叢林中的斑鹿和岩石上的蜥蜴，成為了我的伴侶。兩星期的森林禪修，我感受到生命的簡樸和有如到了極樂淨土一樣的滿足，感恩仁波切慈悲的加持，讓我上了這寶貴的一課。

　　7 月初回港，我開始提筆創作了多篇有關這次閉關的感受的詩，每一份情感都連結着純真無私的愛意，在當下的每一個覺知，擁抱着無垠的脈動。心中的感恩如甘露傾注，奉獻給慈愛一切有情的覺者。7 月下旬，我在臉書上看見一片橘黃的天空就在這個避靜處的上空，原來是加州森林大火漫延此地，面對這場山火的吞噬和後來洪水的洗濯，最後仁波切以一首他寫的詩歌，訴說生命的未知（not knowing），一切的可能性亦因此次山火而躍動。

　　這詩集的緣起只是為了這美好的靜修處的重建經費出一份綿力。感謝出版社黎社長的支持，以最實惠的經費協助出版，還有幫忙修訂英文版本的 TC 和負責中文翻譯的蘇悅，因為兩位妙筆生花，令這本詩集更娓娓動人。最後特別感恩的是心靈導師兼好友阿南渡登仁波切，這三年以來，因緣具足，得到家人和朋友的支持和配合，讓我有機會多次參加他在香港和馬來西亞的閉關和開示，得到他的支持和鼓勵，成就了這本詩集的誕生，亦為我的生命添上一道彩虹！

　　感謝陳志輝院長、陳家玲老師和鄭悅先生，從他們的文字裏，帶領我們感受到與佛陀的邂逅，其實是給與我們重索心靈的機會，面向無條件的大愛與包容，內心迴盪着一份純真之喜悅。最後，感謝香港的家人、美國的親友、如是基金會（Dharmata Foundation）在美國、馬來西亞以及香港各地的同修等，得到大家的支持和配合，讓我這三年安心地往返港、美國和大馬學習佛法和禪修。祈願大家將來亦能到甜水鄉（Sweetwater）親嘗原始森林的氣息，深入生命神聖的殿堂。

何曼盈 寫於香港
2017 年 8 月 27 日

Poem as preface

Bodhi Love on Valentine's Day 2017

Sweetwater

How magical it is

Flaming lips kissed the land

Without destroying it

But it gave you a shock

When you thought the thunderstorms were over

A monstrous flood visited

Without invitation or notice

Rushing from the sky to meet our beloved land

So sorry that it has hurt you, made a tiny scar

Somewhere in your heart

Our giant bodhi tree of Dharmata House

Blesses you for eternity

Whether or not you are free of this pain

Our timid deer and our brave vultures

Came into my mind to send their graceful love to you on this Valentine's Day

They are somewhere in Sweetwater

Safe and sleeping well

詩序
菩提愛在情人節 2017

甜水鄉

多麼奇妙

火焰紅唇親吻大地

沒有完全摧毀

卻讓你如此震驚

當你以為雷暴已過

怪獸般的洪水卻又到訪

不請自來

從天上傾瀉沖向我們心愛的土地

真抱歉，它刺痛了你心中的某個地方

刻下了一道小傷痕

我們如是祇園前的菩提大樹

它永遠守護着你

無論你是否忘卻了這陣傷痛

我們膽小的鹿和勇敢的雄鷹

在這個情人節，來到我心深處，為你送上他們的慈愛

在甜水鄉的某個角落

安好，憩睡着

守望我們再一次的來訪

Waiting for our visit one day

Tina Ho

14-2-2017

Kuala Lumpur, Malaysia

何曼盈
寫於　吉隆坡　馬來西亞
2017 年 2 月 14 日

You Are Just an Ordinary Man

Someone told me
You will bless us
Have confidence in you
Sorry
I do not know what that means
It seems you are the Messiah
It seems you have extraordinary power
Sorry
I cannot imagine that

In my mind
You are just an ordinary man
As ordinary as we are
We have buddha nature
So do you
We have tears and smiles
So do you
We have ordinary mind
So do you
At the same time

你只是一個凡人

有人告訴我
你會加持我們
所以要對你有信心
抱歉！
我無能理解
你似是彌賽亞
你似有非凡的力量
抱歉！
我無法如此想像

在我的腦海裏
你只是一個凡人
和我們一樣平凡
我們具有佛性
你如是
我們有眼淚和微笑
你如是
我們有一顆平常心
你如是
與此同時

We can be blessed by you
Not because you have magical power
But because
I can see you in my heart
Your peaceful smile is just like the shadow in a lake
It opens my heart little by little

Someone says she feels her guru around her
Sorry
I have not had this magical experience
But
I have the power of devotion
It connects us
The more devoted I am, the more I benefit
Benefit how?
My mind becomes more stable
My heart becomes more warm
I am more familiar with my mind
More good qualities emerge

Thanks to you
My life is full of love
My life is full of sacredness
My heart is always dancing
I love you, my heart guru

我們可以被你祝福
不是因為你有神奇的力量
而是
我可以在我的心裏看到你
你平靜的微笑
就像湖中的影子
一點一點地打開我的心

有人說她可以感覺到她的上師就在她身旁
抱歉！
我沒有這種神奇的經驗
但是
我有虔敬之心
它把我們連結在一起
更多的虔敬，更多的靠近
心變得更加穩定
心變得更加溫暖
更熟悉我的心
更多美好的展現

感謝
你讓我的生命有愛
你讓我的生命神聖
你讓我的心舞動
摯誠的上師啊！我愛你

Head to Head

Two years ago
Your head suddenly touched my head
So strange but so warm
I started to cry and cry
I felt you totally allowed me to express my feelings
Now as then

Every time we meet
We will touch head to head
I feel your humility
And I enjoy that moment of connection

Sometimes
We join our heads side by side
In order to take a photo
It is so funny and cute
Just like two kids playing a game
How wonderful it is
We laugh together
And we share our happiness with all the people around us

頭碰頭

兩年前
你的頭突然與我的頭相踫
多麼神奇
多麼溫暖
我不停哭泣
你任由我表達我的感受
從此以後
每當我們見面
我們都會頭踫頭
我感覺你是如此謙虛
我喜歡如此的靠近
有時候
我們側頭相踫
多滑稽，又可愛
就像兩個孩兒嬉戲
多麼美妙
我們一起歡笑
將我們的快樂撒向身邊的人

Hat and Stick

Oh no
We have been apart for just a few months
Yet you have become a lot older
With a walking stick and a hat
I see you walking slowly along the path
My heart breaks

I walk up to you
Ask you why you are using a walking stick
You tell me it is because of your leg
You walk slowly
I follow next to you

You lead us to walk on the Dharma Trail
Even though you need the walking stick
You share it with me going uphill
You hold one end, I hold the other
I follow you at the back

帽子與柺杖

噢！不要
才相隔幾月
你竟然老了
手執一根棍子
頭戴一頂帽子
沿着路徑散步
我的心碎了

我走近了你
「為何要拿着柺杖？」
你說 「腿疼！」
看着你緩緩走來
只有跟隨着你

你引領我們展開旅程
即使你必須依杖而行
你把它與我分享，一起步上坡
你拿着前端，我拿着後端
我在後面跟着你

I do not want to pull too hard
I do not want you to fall down
I walk carefully
We hold the stick together
I follow you at the back

You support me on the Dharma Trail
Back at the starting point
You ask me to use two hands on the stick
So you can pull me up the slope
Our energy is joined together
I follow you at the back

At night
You sit in front of me
And open your heart
You are chanting as a child
Dancing as a snake
I watch you silently
Standing beside you

In the morning
I brew a glass of ginger water for you
We meet on the road
I pass it to you
You drink it without a thought

我不想太用力
不忍讓你摔跤
你一步一腳印
一同拿着枴杖
我就在你身後

你幫助我踏上小徑
當我們重回起點
你要我用雙手拿緊枴杖
一下子
便把我拉上了斜坡
我們彼此能量相融
我就在你身後

夜裏
我倆相對而坐
你的心是開放的
像孩兒在誦經
像靈蛇在起舞
我站在你左右
默默地看着你

清晨
在路上相遇
我為你熬了一杯薑湯
你一飲而盡

I watch you walk with the stick again
I follow next to you

We say goodbye at the backyard of your green house
I watch you take your belongings
And walk slowly to your house
I watch your back
My eyes follow you
Until you reach your home
And disappear in front of me

I stay at the front door of the hall
Waiting to catch a sight of you
You are still wearing your hat
Walking with a stick
We talk a bit
I watch you disappear in front of me

Oh yes
We will be apart for a few months
I will be as beautiful as a dakini
I will see the flower you gave me at morning practice every day
Chanting before the Buddha
Dancing with my whole heart
Walking slowly along the Dharma path
You make my heart blissful

見你手執枴杖往前行走
我跟在你左右

我們在你的綠屋後苑道別
見你拿回衣物
慢慢地步入居所
目送你歸家去
消失了蹤影

在大廳門前
等待你相遇
依然是那一頂帽子
依然是那一根枴杖
打了聲招呼
又漸漸消失了你的蹤影

哦！是的
我們將暫別數月
我將美如空行母
每天看着你送的花做早課
在佛前誦經
全心全意起舞
沿着法道前行
幸福矣！

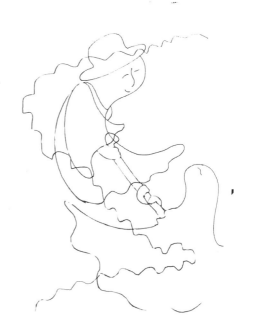

Romancing the Buddha

One day
A few years ago
My friend looked at me and said
You seemed to be dating the Buddha
I laughed
My heart is young

Yesterday
My guru phoned me and said
You seemed to find practice centres romantic
I laughed
My heart is in love

Somewhere in time
A young bodhisattva is dancing in front of the Buddha
They take a lovely photo together
They play, they laugh
They meditate, they immerse themselves in love
They embrace space
A sense of benevolence

與佛陀談情說愛

幾年前
一天
我的朋友望着我說
「你和佛陀相戀！」
我笑了
青春無畏的心

昨天
上師來電說
「你正浪漫於心靈的殿堂」
我笑
心裏泛起濃郁的愛

時光倒流
一位年輕的菩薩在佛陀前舞着
動人的照片
他們玩樂，他們笑
他們禪修，他們愛
他們擁抱虛空
感受着充滿大愛的慈悲

Is touching everyone's hearts

How romantic

Phat!

My guru is ringing the vajra bell

Like a wrathful daka

Urging me back to the day-to-day world

To work for my pension

Shouting at me to wake up

Cutting through my romantic love

Phat!

Come! Cut out my ego

Gods and demons

Sneer at me

Pull me to the cliff's edge

Step on my ignorance and naivety

Push me to jump into the sky

So I may fly to Laputa, the Castle in the Sky

Ah

One full year

I embrace the love

Blossoming in my heart

It is time to leave

Holding on to a scrap of self-esteem

感動着每個人的心
浪漫啊！

吓！
上師擊響金剛鈴
如同忿怒的勇父
督促我回歸現實世界
為退休金而戰鬥
要把我吼醒
要斷除浪漫的愛

吓！
來吧！砍斷我的自我
諸神和心魔
嘲笑我
拖我到懸崖
踐踏我的無知和天真
推我入虛空
飛往天空之城

呀！
三百六十五天
我懷抱着我們所有的愛
心花正怒放
如今是離別的時候
保留卑微的自尊

I end it with a perfect full stop

Giving thanks to all of you

No identity, only gratitude

畫下完美的句點
我向大家道謝
放下身份，
感恩

When I Listen to Your Breath

Day and night

We are apart

The Pacific Ocean divides us

Separating the east from the west

But luckily nowadays

I need only turn on my computer

To swim in the ocean of your breath

Like the waves that come and go on the beach

Your breath is also like the wind of the forest

Blowing from east to west

I listen quietly

Through the audio stereo

My breath dissolves in your breath

Our breaths are chanting together

You and I are one

I can feel your breath

So soft and gentle

Your spirit leading my spirit

Swimming in an ocean

The ocean of love

聽見你的呼吸

日夜交錯
太平洋將我們分割兩地
各分東西
如今慶倖
我只要打開電腦
就能沉浸在你呼吸之海洋裏
如那來回海灘的浪花
你的氣息猶如林中的春風
東來西去
我靜靜通過播放機聆聽
我的氣息消融在你的呼吸裏
一起唸頌
你我合一
我感受着你的氣息
如此柔和溫順
你的心靈引領我的心靈沉浸在愛海裏
那是無別之海
大平等捨之海
世界仿若停止
消失「空」中

The ocean of non-duality

The ocean of equanimity

The world seems to have stopped

It dissolves into nothing

Time has stopped

Only the sound of breathing

One breath after another

Sometimes it is strong

Sometimes it is weak

I follow your breath

Breathing together in harmony

Like the waves that come and go

We are one at this moment

Merged together in eternity

You are always in my heart

Your breath with my breath

We breathe in together

We breathe out together

We live together

時間停頓

只聽見呼吸的聲音

一波一波

時而深沉

時而微細

我隨着你的呼吸

相融於和諧中

猶如海浪般來去

我們此刻為一

相融於恆常中

你長住我心

我倆氣息相連

我們一起吸氣

我們一起呼氣

彼此相融！

This Morning

This morning

After I take refuge in the three gems

I relax and sit on the cushion

Your image arises in my heart

Your words come to me again

I do not need to ask anything of you

You have given me everything

Last year you gave me the steps to enlightenment

Remind me to always stay in awareness

You totally understand me and lead me to bliss

Oh! My heart guru

Our minds are inseparable

I visualise you in my heart and you dissolve in my heart

You are no different from the Buddha, Pemasambhava and Yesol Tsogyel

You lead me to speak what's in my heart

My sorrow and my bliss

今日的晨曦

今日的晨曦

憶念三寶

您的形相浮現我心

您的話語在耳際響起

我無求

您卻無私給予

您引領我踏上開悟之道

您引領我進入覺性之海

您懂我，明瞭我所需的幸福

噢！摯誠的上師

您是如此靠近

無二無別

您是佛陀，是蓮師，是移喜措嘉

您聽懂我心中的話

幸福與哀愁

Every Time I See You

Every time I see you
In your eyes
I see your warmth
I see your loving-kindness
I see your compassion

Every time I hear you
In your voice
I hear your silence
I hear your calmness
I hear your wisdom

每一次看您

每一次看您
在您深深的雙眸裏
有溫暖
有慈愛
有悲心

每一次聽您
在您動人的聲音裏
有寂靜
有祥和
有般若

Your Words

I love your words
They are silent
But they touch my heart

They are as beautiful as butterflies
As sweet as honey
They make my heart dance
They open my heart
My inspiration, nectar-like
Pours from my heart

Pages and pages are written
From notes taken at dharma teachings
And as I reflect on my dance practice
Poetry softens my heart
And lets a rainbow shine forth
Beautiful and colourful

你的話語

喜歡你的話語
他們如斯沉默
卻觸動了我的心弦

他們美豔如蝶
如蜜一般香甜
他們舞動了我的心弦
敞開了我的心靈
我的靈感
像泉湧
從心中流淌而出

一篇一篇
佛法的讚頌
舞蹈之回顧
詩歌融化了我的心
尤如彩虹
絢麗奪目

Oh! Big Tree

Oh! Big tree

Today I lie down to look at you

Your leaves cover me gently

Like an umbrella

I once gave to him

He opened it with a big smile

He looked at every part of it

The dharma-red colour suits him

He can bring the umbrella all over the world

It can protect him from heavy rain

I was so happy he accepted it with no objection

Loving-kindness spread from our hearts in that moment

Like the nectar from Avalokiteśvara's vase

He loves us more than we love him

It is unconditional

He embraces everything in front of him

Rejecting nothing

Oh! Big tree

You embrace me with your green leaves

大樹

大樹！

我仰望着你

你綠色的衣裳掩護了我

像是我送給他的雨傘

他微笑把雨傘撐開

細細觀看

藏紅是他的顏色

陪伴他行走世界各個角落

擋風抵雨

欣喜他收下

此時我倆心中充滿着慈愛

恰如觀世音淨瓶裏的甘露

我們愛他

他更愛我們

沒有條件

沒有否定

他擁抱一切

沒有拒絕

大樹！

They seem like a piece of clothing

Sewn with many diamonds

Sparkling in the sky

It covers me softly

I fall into the dharma land of Guru Rinpoche

Chanting his mantra

Sleeping on his bed

Nearby your roots

Om Ah Hung Vajra Guru Pema Siddhi Hung!

The chant connects me with Padmasambhava

And through Padmasambhava, we are joined

He is my guide

Who leads me on the Dharma Trail

With his support

I go beyond fear and non-fear

I follow his pace

He lets me hold on to his walking stick

We walk together

I feel his energy

Push me up the slope

We reach the destination

And start again

Oh! Big tree

I am chanting the mantra of the Heart Sūtra

Cover me with your vajra leaves

你綠色的衣裳掩護了我

仿如一片綉滿鑽石的綢緞

閃爍於天空

掩蓋着我

我置身於蓮師之淨土

唱誦他的歌

酣睡在他的溫床

貼近你心深處

「嗡啊吽，班渣 咕嚕 啤瑪 悉地吽！」

它讓我們緊緊相連

他，我的嚮導

隨他踏上法道路

因他的教誨及無私

讓我超越了恐懼的有無

只要隨着他的步伐

我倆一起拿着他的拐杖

沒有分離

往前走

他激盪的能量

把我推上斜坡

到了終點

重回起點

大樹！

我唸誦着《心經》的梵咒

你金剛般的綠葉掩護着我

I see your form

And I see your emptiness

You are dancing with the wind

Singing holy songs

He sits on the stairs in front of the holy temple

Wearing shoes

That have taken him all over the world

Spreading the truth of the dharma

I sit beside him

We are talking about languages

He wants to learn more

So he can converse in Chinese

I show him again and again

The intonation of the words

He listens carefully

Full of patience

We read the words together

It gives me an opportunity to stay with him longer

It was a memorable moment

More beautiful than any words can be

Oh! Big tree

You are the witness of such unconditional love

Please memorise this moment

Keep it deep in your heart

Chanting in the wind

我見你的形影

在虛空中舞動

唱誦神聖之歌

他坐在聖殿前的階梯

把鞋穿上

這鞋陪他走天涯

遍處弘法

我倆談論中文

與華人對話，是他的心願

我一遍遍地重複

文辭的語調

他用心聆聽

耐心隨我唸

珍惜與他單獨相處

這是美麗的回憶

超越文字之美麗

大樹！

你是大愛之見証者

請記得這一刻

寄存在你心裏

唱詠在風中

Smile

Every day I see you in my heart
Your smile calms me
It is so warm and charming
Your energy spreads like the warmth of sunshine
Shining on a gurgling brook
It makes the refreshing water warm
Birds and butterflies flying around small streams
The green grass tasting the nectar-like water

You wear Tibetan red clothes with a beige shawl
Sitting on the rocks
Looking far away
The blue sky with white clouds in front of you
They are changing

You just look and smile
Under your big hat
You are present in each moment

微笑

您的面容在我心中搖曳
您的微笑總令我感覺平靜
多麼溫馨迷人
您就像那暖和的陽光
照耀着淙淙的溪流
溪水不再冰冷
鳥兒蝴蝶都來了
展姿飛舞
清泉潤濕了小草

您一身藏紅
米色的披肩
端坐在岩石上
遙望着
遠方那白雲藍天
如此無常幻變

您僅僅見證着
在大帽底下，一副笑臉
你遍在一切生靈之處

Embracing every creature

Every tiny flower gives you pleasure

The wind kisses your face

And embraces you with the warmest regards

每一朵小花都能讓你歡顏
風輕撫你的臉
以熱切的問候擁抱着你

Flying Dakini

It is time to take a break

We leave this Sweetwater place

On the road

You take a nap

Seeing that you have fallen asleep

I remember I have a sleeping pillow in my bag

I fill it with air

But I don't want to disturb your sweet dreams

At this moment

You wake up with a jolt

It is a good time to pass you the pillow

You accept it and fall into sleep again

You must be very tired

For you have travelled so much in the past few weeks

You had just come back to join the retreat

You will stay for two days before leaving again

I sit in the back seat

I watch you sleep

And hope that you sleep well

飛行中的空行母

離開了斯威特沃特
車漸行漸遠
在車廂裏，是時候歇一歇
見你隨着累意入眠
咿！想起我的背包裏的睡枕
我立即把它吹滿了氣
我又害怕打擾你的甜夢
忽然
你微微一顫醒來
我把睡枕傳遞給你

你接過，把枕睡去
這日夜的奔波
您必定累了
感謝你到甜水鄉來
兩天後你將離去
真不忍見你勞心費力
在這車廂裏
我只有靜靜守望着你
願你安享在甜蜜的睡鄉裏

I practise the mudra for the White Tara vajra dance

It is so peaceful in the car

I do my practice

You sleep in calmness

David drives us in awareness

In this moment

We are just like a dakini flying in the sky

You wake up again

And thank us for our patience

You are so humble

This is what I should learn from you

When you chanted at a ceremony to mark the opening of Sweetwater

You thanked the land

For allowing us to use this beautiful land

Are there any spirits in the land?

Do they really exist?

I do not think like that

These are questions that will come up in a religious or scientific argument

However

When I go deep into the essence of the act of thanks

I see the great humility behind

You are humble before the land

Grateful to all things

All these things act as a support

我默默修持白度母
車廂裏瀰漫着一股寧靜
我修持白度母的金剛舞手印
你安然歇息在寂靜裏
大偉覺知地駕駛

這時候
我們恰如空行母翱翔天際
你再次從熟睡中醒來
用真實謙恭的心向我們道謝
你是我們修行的依怙
當你為了斯威特沃特加持唸頌
讚頌感恩那片美麗土地的允許
土地真有神祇？
我確實有點兒懷疑
這些將顯現為印度教或科學的論證

打從心底感動
你對土地及一切的敬重及謙卑
以它們作為你修持的伴侶
在空性裏，它們是如此幻化不實
道路上的汽車展示如精靈
你喜悅地親吻我們坐駕的儀錶板
你顯得實在太可愛
我會記裏你最人性化的指引
在佛教的傳記裏

For practising humility

They are not real but full of emptiness

You elaborate it in a lovely way

You say the cars on the roads are all spirit

You kiss the car dashboard joyfully

This is the second time you are so cute in this retreat

I will remember your guidance

Dharma in the most simple, human terms

In the world of religion

There are so many deities and dakinis that I sometimes get confused

Tonight

There are so many stars sparkling in the sky

They are just like the spirits of dakinis

Listening to my heart

I see a falling star

Sweep across the sky

I go out of my room

To find a spot where I can see more stars

I sleep on the same bench you slept on one night

The big tree with sparkling stars hanging in the sky

I imagine we are inseparable

Dissolving into the same space

I go back to my bedroom

My window has the widest view to see the stars

記載了無數的本尊、勇父和空行
真的令我有點迷惑

今天夜裏
繁星在天空中閃爍着
如同眾空行母的展現
聆聽着我內心的聲音
我彷彿看見那空行母
飛往天際
我拔腿往外奔去
尋找更多劃破天際的明星
仰躺在你那一夜睡過的板凳上
那棵大樹的頂上掛着朵朵星光
我們彼此無有分離
消融在同一虛空裏
我返回寢室
此處窗兒寬敞，看見繁星熠熠
一顆流星劃過

消失於空中
不見了蹤影
我祈願
在夢
與你再次相遇

I see a meteor fall

I make a wish at once

As it disappears

I make a wish to see you in my dreams

Chocolate Night

I have come here

Because of your sincere invitation

Even though I never thought I would go to the US

Yet here I am in this Sweetwater hermitage

You guided me to open up my world

Cross the ocean

To reach the pure land

You prepared this comfortable place for us

I can relax my mind

It is so simple

So peaceful and harmonious

Chanting, practising, meditating and dancing

At night

We enjoy the dharma

Practising in a non-traditional way

You created an American Sūtra:

"We hear what we want to hear, we don't hear what we don't want to hear."

You chant and chant

Wishing us to be aware of each word

巧克力之夜

我的到來
是您盛情的邀請
在那以前，美國只是個夢
現在處身於斯威特沃特冬宮
您打開了我的世界
橫渡海洋
登陸淨土
您貼心安排了此淨地
任我放鬆心情
我心中的步伐如斯簡單
這般和諧
隨意自在
唸誦，修持，舞動

夜裏
我啜飲佛法甘露
多姿多彩
您創作美國真言「聽你想聽的，不聽你不想聽的」
您重複唸着

You created "Om hamburger svaha"

Chanting and patting a pack of chocolates in rhythm

We laugh and laugh

You use these different methods to try to awaken us

You are so lovely

Like a child always

Repeating and repeating

You open up your mind

You tell the truth

You answer our requests

Dancing a vajra dance with a Native American rattle

You whirl and whirl

Beyond hopes and fears

You enjoy being in awareness

You embrace the nature of mind

You sleep under the big tree

Lie on a red wooden bench

Resting under the moon and stars

Nature embraces you

You seem like a baby sleeping sweetly

Your compassion spreads to the tip of each branch

Touching our hearts

害怕我們會遺忘

您創作「唵！漢堡包，娑婆訶！」

一面唸頌一面敲打着巧克力包

逗樂了我們

見您善巧想要喚醒我們

您是如此純真

像是孩兒一樣

持續開啓您的心門

向人們訴說真實

回應眾生的訴求

揮動着美洲土著的沙錘

沉浸金剛舞之中

旋轉再旋轉

超越了期望和恐懼

安享在覺知

懷抱着心性

睡在大樹底

躺在紅木板凳上

您仰臥在月亮與星辰之下

任由自然懷抱着您

甜蜜睡着，像初生的嬰兒

您的慈悲延伸到枝頭

觸動了我們的心靈

Heart is Emptiness; Emptiness is Heart

My heart guru

When I leave you one day from this world

Please do not feel too much sorrow

You are a good poet

You are so sensitive

I will be a rainbow

It is so beautiful

It will appear sometimes

Sending you all the bliss;

I will be the wind

Telling you fairy tales when you sit in the hermitage;

I will be the air

Melting in you when you breathe;

I will be the ocean

Connecting in energy with you;

I will be the snow

Decorating your place of retreat in white;

心即空 · 空如心

摯誠的上師啊！
若有一天我離這世界而去
請別悲傷
我知道
您有着詩人的靈敏

我願化為一道美麗的彩虹
當它出現
給您獻上無限的祝福
當您獨坐冬宮
我願為一陣風
給您講述我的童話故事
當您呼息時
我願化為空氣
我消融在您之中
我化為浩瀚的海洋
與您的能量相融
當您獨自閉關時
我願化為白雪
為您鋪蓋純白的裝飾

I will be the grass

On which you sleep in front of the shrine;

I will be the roses

Sending my love to you.

It is so beautiful

I transform into other forms

Sending prayers and blessings to you!

Many thanks to Wincy Wong, a fellow student of Rinpoche's, for setting this poem to song

我願化為廟前的草坪
供您仰躺歇息
我願化為玫瑰
把我的愛意傳送給你

美！這幻化之身
承載着對您的愛與祝福！

感謝仁波切的學生王詠思為這首詩寫成歌曲

My Deer

My deer

I do not know how much I love you

Someone told me that

One day

You stood beside my heart guru

As he took a nap

In this restful garden

They said that the scene reminded them of the Buddha taking a rest

And you

My deer

You were so beautiful standing by his side

I think

This sounds just like Sārnāth, the deer park in Buddha's time

A few days later

I went down to your holy place

I wore a long-sleeved shirt

And a big hat to protect me from the shining sun

I held a long mop

And was cleaning the swimming pool

我的鹿

鹿
我不知道我有多愛你
他們說
一天
當摯誠的上師於此地休憩
你守護在他的身旁
美極了，這畫面！
令人憶起鹿野苑

幾日後的思念
我來到這片神聖的土地
一身白襯衫
一頂大草帽
清理着那被遺棄的泳池

一面唸頌蓮師心咒
忽然我發現
你躲在叢林中

As before
I was chanting the Padmasambhava mantra
Suddenly I heard some noise from the bush
I found
You hiding behind some woods
You were so beautiful
You were still very young
You did not have antlers on your head
I carried on chanting
I looked at you
And you looked at me
You stayed there for a while
And you disappeared

Lately
You have been on my mind
I worry about you
Are you all right?
The fire has been burning from the north to the south
Did you run to the other parts of the forest?
It is unknown

Today I saw a picture
Of the place where we met
It has been ruined by the fire
All the wooden furniture turned to ash

多美啊你！
青春的年華
我持續唱頌
如此凝望着彼此
瞬間
你消失了蹤影

我還在思念着你
牽掛於你
你，好嗎？
無情的大火北焚南燒
你會不會逃到另一個叢林裏去？
沒人知曉

今天我看見一幅照片
我們相遇之地成了廢墟
泳池依然還在
你躲藏的草叢依然油綠
你在哪裏？
你，可好嗎？
沒人知曉

我尋覓你的蹤影

I could see the swimming pool
I could see the bush that hid you
Where are you now?
Are you all right?
It is unknown

I search for you in my heart
I do not know how much I love you
In my heart you are standing calmly
You are looking at me
And I am looking at you
May you be safe
May you be alive
I send my warmest regards to you

我不知道我有多愛你
在我心中佇立
如此凝望着彼此
祈願你平安
寄予你深邃的祝福

Thanks for Waiting for Us

Thanks for waiting for us
You always take care of us
In the day or in the night
You are just like a huge rock
Standing in the middle of the road
Waiting for the whole group
To find the right way

You move
No matter how dark it is
You are present
Moving with ease
I look at your back
How huge you are
Like a mountain straddling the ocean
I can sense your movement without seeing
How fast you move
Like the winter leaves blowing in space

Light appears

感謝您的守候

感謝您的守候
您的眷顧
不論白天，還是黑夜
您如同一塊佇立在路邊的巨石
等待着我們
指引前方的道路

無論前方有多黑暗
您勇往直前
在這當下
我望着您的背影
您雄偉如海洋上的一座山巒
我能感覺您的移動
在虛空中
輕盈如風中冬葉

燈火通明
亮了林中小徑
一地橘黃
照亮了我們的倒影

Further up the trail

Turning the trail into orange

It gives us warmth and shadows

A dark shadow lies on the road

It's yours

We follow your steps

We follow your shadow

No fear, only joy

"gate gate pāragate pārasaṃgate bodhi svāhā"

The sound of our chanting rises

We are chanting in the dark

Like a group of dakinis

Ringing their bells in the sky

It is so lovely

Melting into your voice

看！您的倒影

隨着您的腳步穿梭而行

只有喜悅

沒有恐懼

「揭諦，揭諦，波羅揭諦，波羅僧揭諦，菩提薩婆訶！」

這黑暗之中的廻響

有如空行母

在虛空中搖晃金鈴

如此美妙

消融在您的音聲裏

White Tara Offering

This morning

I visualise White Tara

Chanting her vajra dance song

I feel her soft embrace

With my whole body

My mind, my voice

Singing as soft as she is

A 16-year-old bodhisattva

Dancing in the temple

I offer my body, speech and mind to you

In union with our bliss

Tonight is the last night

I meditate in the temple

The sky becomes darker and darker

Only my breathing can be heard

Time comes

I stand in front of the White Tara thangka

I am dressed in pure white, inside and out

A silk dress printed with pink lotuses

白度母獻供

晨曦的觀想
唱誦白度母的金剛咒曲
她是如此柔順
擁抱着我的身軀
我的音聲和意念
如同她般溫柔
仿如十六歲的妙音天女
在寺內翩翩起舞
我的身口意奉獻給您
與她的幸福
融合一體

這最後一夜
我在寺內靜修
黑夜漸漸來臨
只聽見呼吸的低吟

暮鐘響了
我佇立在白度母的唐卡前
白色如天

Covers my body softly

I start to chant the song

The singing is so sweet

The dancing is so pretty

My hands are just like the wings of butterfly

Flying among the lotuses

My feet are like white snakes

Whirling on the grass

I offer the White Tara vajra dance to the hermitage

With love and blessing

I would love to offer the dance to you also

One day

When the time comes

I will offer it to you

蓮一般的絲綢裙擺

掩映着我的身體

唱吧！

甜美的歌聲

舞吧！

像那蝴蝶

在蓮花叢中翩翩起舞

我雙腳如白蛇般

蜿蜒在草地上

供養白度母之舞予冬宮

散發愛與祝福

有那麼一天

我也把此舞

奉獻給您

A Song of the Blue Bird

Blue bird, blue bird

Do you know you are special to me?

The first time we met

Near the big tree

While I was practising in this forest

I saw you flying before me

I was so excited

Because here is a legend

No one has seen a blue bird before

Everyone searches for it everywhere

But it is actually in their home

I watched a Broadway performance about you last Christmas

I loved that opera

Those two weeks I was in retreat

I saw you in front of me

I was so happy

You and your family were singing in the forest

I heard you every day

You knocked on my door when I was meditating in the temple yurt

You knocked on my roof in the morning when I was still lying in bed

青鳥之歌

青鳥
你是如此獨特
我們初次相遇在森林中
正當我在靜修之際
我看見你一飛而過
如此振奮人心
傳說中沒有人看見過青鳥
每個人到處尋找
原來你就在家中
去年聖誕，我看了百老滙歌劇《青鳥》
讓我如斯着迷
十四天的獨處靜修期間
有你的出現
令我快樂無比
我聽見
你敲響我的關房
踏響屋瓦的聲音
喚醒我懶洋洋的身體
多想拍攝下你的美麗
你十分警覺

I tried to take a photo of you

But you were so alert

I walked carefully on the Dharma Trail

I ran after you to the forest of thorns

You were hiding up in the trees

You played hide and seek with me

Today you are still playing with me

I find no trace of you

The fire ruined our sanctuary

No one can go into this hermitage area

We cannot listen to your singing again

Where are you?

You can fly

You must be hiding somewhere

Taking a rest with your family

The air is full of smoke

I pray that you are alright

The fire will soon be entirely extinguished

Please be patient

Everything will be peaceful again

We will meet again

We will listen to your singing again in this sacred place

我小心翼翼到法徑
你卻躲進荊棘林中
和我玩捉迷藏

今天，不見你的踪影
無情之火焚化了甜水鄉
暫別遠離
不再聽見你的吟唱
那煙火瀰漫
你在何方？
快躲！與你的眷屬找個安全之地
我為你禱告
請耐心等待
火終將熄滅
我倆又會再次故地重逢
在你動人的歌聲裏

Transformation in Love

This morning
I stand in front of you calmly
Waiting for my turn
Your hand reaches out gently
To invite me to sit down
We touch our foreheads together in greeting
I listen to your chanting
Blessing me
"Ah Ahh Sha Sa Ma Ha"
I feel the vibration in your head
I enjoy this moment
You love me unconditionally
I hear it in your voice
I love you, too
You bless me with a small bunch of flowers
Reminding me the true way of the dharma
Just like the Buddha transmitting the dharma to his disciple
You and I are connected
From now on
I offer you my body, speech and mind

愛的幻化

今晨
我站在您面前
如此安靜
您伸出那柔和的手臂
邀請我坐下
我倆西藏式的碰了額頭
我微微聽見您在為我唸誦
「阿 阿 夏 沙 瑪 哈！」
您內在強烈的能量激盪着我的心
聽您愛的吟唱
享受着您無私的愛意
我也如此愛着您
您以小花祝福
指引我踏上成佛之路
就像是佛陀把心意傳給了他的繼承人
從今以後
我們無二無別
我以身口意供養您
與您走在成佛之道上
徜徉在覺性之中

In the dharma way
Walking in awareness

Tonight
I embrace my own body
Free from any bounds
It is as perfect as Machig Labdrön
I dance and dance
With perfect pose and blissful mind
I offer all the dances to you
With love and gratitude

Oh your love
Raises my mind to the pure land
Frees my body from all boundaries
Lets me sing like a bird
Lets my mind fly in the blue sky
My body comes from nature
Now it is embraced by nature
The water purifying my body seems like lotus nectar
The wind feels like a shawl
Covering my skin from the crown of my head to the tip of my toes
I bathe in sunshine
It is so awesome

今夜
我懷抱着身軀
沒有束縛
如同瑪姬拉尊的體態
舞動着幸福
獻給您衷心的感恩及愛意

啊！您的愛
讓我沉浸在淨土裏
身是自由
聲如鳥鳴
心遨遊藍天
我身與自然相擁
淨化於蓮花甘露
包裹於縷縷清風
沐浴於午間豔陽
妙極！

Roses and Forget-me-nots

Roses, roses

How charming you are

You are blossoming as a young lady

Dressed in a pink skirt

Soft and light

Welcome, our honourable guest

You stand beside our sacred masters

Listening to our chanting

In this moment of chöd practice

Forget-me-nots

I did not forget you

Your purple is a match with the pink

Soft and light

Dancing with the pink roses

Welcome, our companions

You sit under the hem of the roses

Listening to our guru's guidance

In this moment of meditation practice

玫瑰蜜語

啊！玫瑰
您這般
像十六歲的少女
一身粉紅的羅裳
微風徐徐
來吧！我的妃子
依偎在聖者的身旁
聽吧！那施身法的吟誦

勿忘我
我不曾忘記您
您一身粉紫
與玫瑰相印共舞
去吧！成為伴侶
依坐在玫瑰的裙擺下
聆聽上師的法語
進入禪意

Venerable Dorje Lopön

You always appear in our mind

You are so warm and soft

You never forget us

Always sending us love and compassion

Your love is the amrita pouring into our hearts

We bathe in a sea of unconditional love

The echo of taking refuge in the three treasures

Makes my voice so stereoscopic

My voice sounds

As if I am resting in emptiness space

Aware of each word

Connecting with the dharma

Chanting in melodious sadhana

Resting in a peaceful mind

啊！金剛上師

您不離我們的心

您這般溫順

不曾把我們忘記

您的愛與慈悲

經已注滿了我們的心靈

讓我們沐浴在無私的愛海裏

皈依三寶的吟唱

響徹大地

安住在法界裏

覺知每個字句

與佛法相連

吟誦成就法的旋律

休息於平和的心中

The Tips Of Our Fingers

It was time to leave

We had flown to the sacred land where you will preach

At the entrance of the gate

You asked us to come near

We said goodbye as usual

Head to head and palms to palms

Except the tips of our fingers

You reached out your hands and touched my fingers

I feel something

But I say nothing

Just hide it in my heart

At midnight

I search my memory

The tips of our fingers emerge in my heart

I google some words

A song appears in front of me

You hold me right on the tip of your fingers

You let my love slip through your hands

It's a long, long way from the tip of your fingers

指尖蜜語

是時候離開了
飛往你傳道的聖地
在大閘的入口
你要我們走近
我們像往常一樣道別
頭踫頭，掌並掌
我們的指尖相連
你碰觸我的指尖
那感覺
我什麼都沒說
只隱藏在我的心間

這午夜
那一幕又重現
我試着在網絡上拼寫一些單詞
一首古老的歌曲出現在我眼前
你把我握在你的手指尖上
你讓我的愛滑過你的雙手
這是一道悠長的路，從你的指尖

To the love hidden deep in my heart

You know everything

But you say nothing

Just hide it in your heart

滑過深藏在我心中的愛
你知道一切
但你什麼也沒說
只是隱藏在你的心間

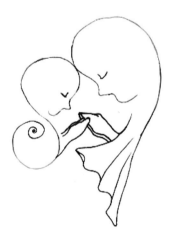

Postscript
Live News from the Mountains

Orion inspires the romantic imagination that all is alive.

The Milky Way is like a road for celestials to travel on

and to drink the endless cosmic wonder.

The nearby creek sings a gentle lullaby for my sweet dream.

In the living trees, who communicate with the language of spirit,

happily wandering creatures do what they want.

I'm alone here.

Wind, sky, clouds, smells, earth, rock,

this is all I got.

No more shame of my body,

I feel like primordial innocence is regained.

Pants and belt look weird.

I had to laugh at them uncontrollably,

especially at the thing called underwear.

Redwoods don't own bank accounts.

All redwoods are simply redwoods.

Not even one redwood says "I am richer than that redwood".

The red madrone makes no claim of being more beautiful than that little bush.

Wild poppies seem happy to see me.

跋
來自山上的直播

獵戶座激發浪漫的想像力，
一切生意盎然，
銀河是天使的通道，
在此暢飲宇宙的奧妙。
鄰近的小溪為我的美夢低吟溫柔的搖籃曲。
充滿靈性的林子中，
生靈快樂地遊蕩，隨心所欲
我獨自在此，
風，天空，雲，氣味，大地，岩石，
只有他們與我同在，
我的身體不再感到羞恥，
我重拾天真無邪
褲子和皮帶看起來好怪
我無法停止笑話它們
還有那叫做內衣的勞什子。
紅杉沒有銀行賬戶。
所有的紅杉都只是紅杉。
沒有一棵紅杉說「我比那株紅杉更富有」
紅色的野草莓沒有聲稱比那個小灌木更美麗。

They offer me the nicest smile to warm my little frozen heart.

This new bliss is overflowing,

It is a sea whirling inside me,

I'm right now swimming in it.

I'm the sea and the swimmer.

Comparison,

Competition,

Greed,

Judgment,

Shame,

I don't know where they went.

Either they dissolved into a black hole,

or they are on a temporary sabbatical.

I'm held in the indescribable benevolence of the universe.

Invisible forces tell me that I'm complete.

This is the first time I feel that every cell in my body is sacred.

This is the report from one night's expedition into the mountains.

I hope you all come here to see this.

This

This

By Anam Thubten Rinpoche, written during his retreat at the Sweetwater Hermitage in Big Sur

野罌粟花似乎很高興見到我

他們給我最好的微笑，以溫暖我冰凍的心。

新的快樂洋溢

如海洋旋轉在我身心

我遨遊在此

無大海與泳者之分。

攀比，

競爭，

貪婪，

判斷，

恥辱，

我不知道他們去了哪裏

或許他們溶入黑洞，

或許他們暫時休假。

宇宙以其難以言表的仁慈懷抱着我，

無形的力量告訴我，我是圓滿的

我第一次覺得我身體裏的每個細胞都是神聖的。

這是進山一夜的報導。

我希望你們都能來這裏見證這個

這個

這個

（中文翻譯提供自美國）

阿南渡登仁波切於閉關中心（Sweetwater Hermitage in Big Sur），有感而作

Dancing in My Heart 舞動心弦

作　　者：Tina Ho 何曼盈
責任編輯：黎漢傑
美術設計：鄒雪兒
內文插圖：何曼盈
法律顧問：陳煦堂 律師

出　　版：初文出版社有限公司
　　　　　電郵：manuscriptpublish@gmail.com

印　　刷：陽光（彩美）印刷公司

發　　行：香港聯合書刊物流有限公司
　　　　　香港新界大埔汀麗路 36 號
　　　　　中華商務印刷大廈 3 字樓
　　　　　電話 (852) 2150-2100 傳真 (852) 2407-3062

臺灣總經銷：貿騰發賣股份有限公司
　　　　　地址：新北市中和區中正路 880 號 14 樓
　　　　　電話：886-2-82275988
　　　　　傳真：886-2-82275989
　　　　　網址：www.namode.com

版　　次：2017 年 9 月初版
國際書號：978-988-78270-9-2
定　　價：港幣 68 元 新臺幣 210 元

Published and printed in Hong Kong

香港印刷及出版